Showdown at the Yo-Yo Corral

Written by Scott Peterson
Based on the series created by Dan Povenmire & Jeff "Swampy" Marsh

Printed in the United States of America   First Edition   1 3 5 7 9 10 8 6 4 2

ISBN 978-1-4231-4802-9

J689-1817-1-12075

For more Disney Press fun, visit www.disneybooks.com

Disney Press
New York

It WAS A WARM, SUNNY DAY IN DANVILLE when Phineas and Ferb's friend Buford strode into their backyard.

"Look what I got last week," he bragged as he took out a flashy, new yo-yo. "I'm probably the best yo-yo'er in the whole Tri-State Area. Minus the *probably*."

Phineas and Ferb's sister, Candace, was watching the yo-yo-ing from her bedroom window.

"I can't believe Phineas and Ferb are playing with lame little kiddie toys today," she complained to her mom on the phone. "They're not building outer-space volcanoes or robot gorillas or doing *anything* bustable!"

"Boys playing. That IS unusual," her mother said dryly. "Now, I'm about to start my advanced origami class and won't be able to answer my phone. This is your last chance to freak out and beg me to come home."

Don't worry.

Apparently **NOTHING** is happening here today.

But Candace was wrong. Something exciting was happening. Phineas had just come up with a great idea!

"There's only one way to settle this," Phineas said to Ferb and Buford, as he watched them showing off their yo-yo techniques. "An old-fashioned, high noon, man-to-man yo-yo showdown. Ferb, I know what you're gonna do today!"

I suppose flipping a coin is out of the question?

Phineas grinned. This was going to be the best day of summer vacation ever! He looked around to tell his pet platypus, Perry, the news. But he couldn't find Perry anywhere.

Little did Phineas know that Perry had just transformed into Agent P to try to stop the evil (and highly predictable) Dr. Doofenshmirtz. But Agent P was quickly captured by his nemesis, as usual.

"Behold!" Dr. Doofenshmirtz cried. "My Giganta-Pogo-inator! With this, the world's largest pogo stick, I will bounce around Danville, distracting the easily amused public and captivating their attention."

Candace was in the kitchen when she suddenly heard a loud noise outside. As she peered out the window, she couldn't believe her eyes. "They built a western town in our backyard? In fifteen minutes?" she cried. She ran outside, dodging mechanical horses and wagons as she called her mom.

"No answer," Candace moaned. "That's right! Mom is stuck in her silly paper-wrinkling class. This couldn't get any worse."

As Candace continued to run through the western town, a horse bumped into her. It knocked her into a puddle and splashed her with mud. Before she could get up, the horse sat right on top of her!

As the clock tower struck noon, the kids headed to the center of the town. Ferb and Buford slowly moved toward each other, their spurs clinking in the dust.

"Let the showdown begin!" Phineas cheered.

Isabella and Baljeet watched nervously. Who would be the winner?

The two competitors showed off their sophisticated yo-yo tricks such as the classic "Walking the Dog," along with some newly invented ones they called "Looping the Linoleum" and "Flushing the Filigree." Each trick was better than the last!

At the same time, Dr. Doofenshmirtz had just climbed into the cockpit atop his gigantic pogo stick and started to wave good-bye to Perry. But the platypus had escaped!

WHAM! Suddenly, Agent P leaped toward the evil doctor. Fighting in the cockpit, the two enemies began to bounce wildly around Danville!

Knocking Dr. Doofenshmirtz out of the cockpit, Agent P lunged for the control panel on the pogo stick and threw it into overdrive.

"No!" Dr. Doofenshmirtz howled. "Not overdrive! Why did I even include that option?" The pogo stick bounced back and forth uncontrollably.

Back in the western town, the showdown was heating up. Ferb's tricks were so fancy that Buford started to get nervous.

Refusing to be defeated, Buford performed more and more difficult tricks in order to outdo Ferb.

Huh?!?

"There's no winning or losing among masters," Ferb told Buford. "I was only defending my yo-yo honor, just like you were, pardner." The friends shook hands.

At that moment, the horse that had used Candace as a resting spot finally decided to move along, freeing her from the mud puddle. As she pulled herself up from the muck, she heard her mom's car pull into the driveway. She leaped over a hitching post and raced toward her mom.

BOING! The pogo stick catapulted back up into the air with the squashed town stuck to the bottom of it. But everyone was so busy practicing with their yo-yos they didn't even notice!

Candace's mom peered into the backyard and sighed.

"Okay, Candace," her mother said. "What part of playing cowboys would you like me to bust them for? And why are you so muddy?"

As the pogo stick bounced away, Perry dove off and launched his parachute. Dr. Doofenshmirtz spiraled into his headquarters and the pogo stick shattered!

Dr. Doofenshmirtz groaned. Agent P had foiled the evil doctor's plan to dominate the Tri-State Area—again!